This Walker book belongs to:

....

....

....

For Gabriel

First published 2017 by Walker Books Ltd
87 Vauxhall Walk, London SE11 5HJ

This edition published 2017

4 6 8 10 9 7 5

© 2017 Lucy Cousins

The right of Lucy Cousins to be identified as author/illustrator of this work has been
asserted by her in accordance with the Copyright, Designs and Patents Act 1988.

Handlettering by Lucy Cousins.

Printed in China

British Library Cataloguing in Publication Data:
a catalogue record for this book is available from the British Library.

ISBN 978-1-4063-7654-8

www.walker.co.uk

MIX
Paper from
responsible sources
FSC® C144853
FSC
www.fsc.org

A Busy Day for Birds

Lucy Cousins

WALKER BOOKS
AND SUBSIDIARIES
LONDON · BOSTON · SYDNEY · AUCKLAND

Can you imagine...
just for one day...
you're a busy bird?

Yes, a bird!

Hooray!

The sun is up,
the sky is blue.
Wake up and shout

Cock-a-
doodle-
doo!

The sun is up,
the sky is blue.
Wake up and shout

Cock-a-
doodle-
doo!

Flap your wings
and you can **fly**,
higher and higher,
up, up in the sky.

Hop, hop, hop!

Now swim along
and
stretch
up
your
neck.

Say
"Hello darling."

Then swoop like a starling.

Swoop
up

and
down,

Swoop round and round.

Catch a fly with your beak.

Stand
very
tall
on
just
one
leg.

Say

"Cluck cluck!"

and lay an egg.

Catch
a
wriggly
snake

and
stretch
out
your
wings.

Waddle like a penguin
in the snow.

Show off your tail

and
wiggle
your
bum.

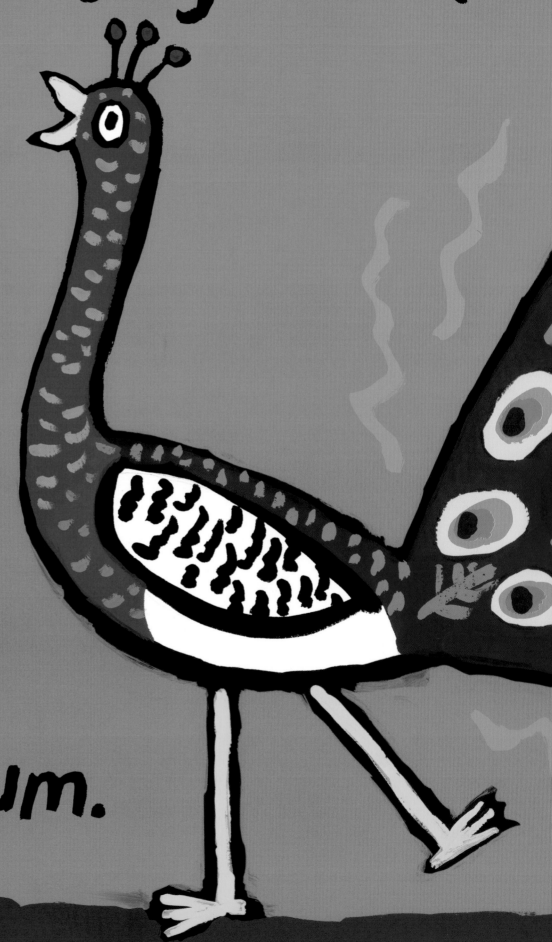

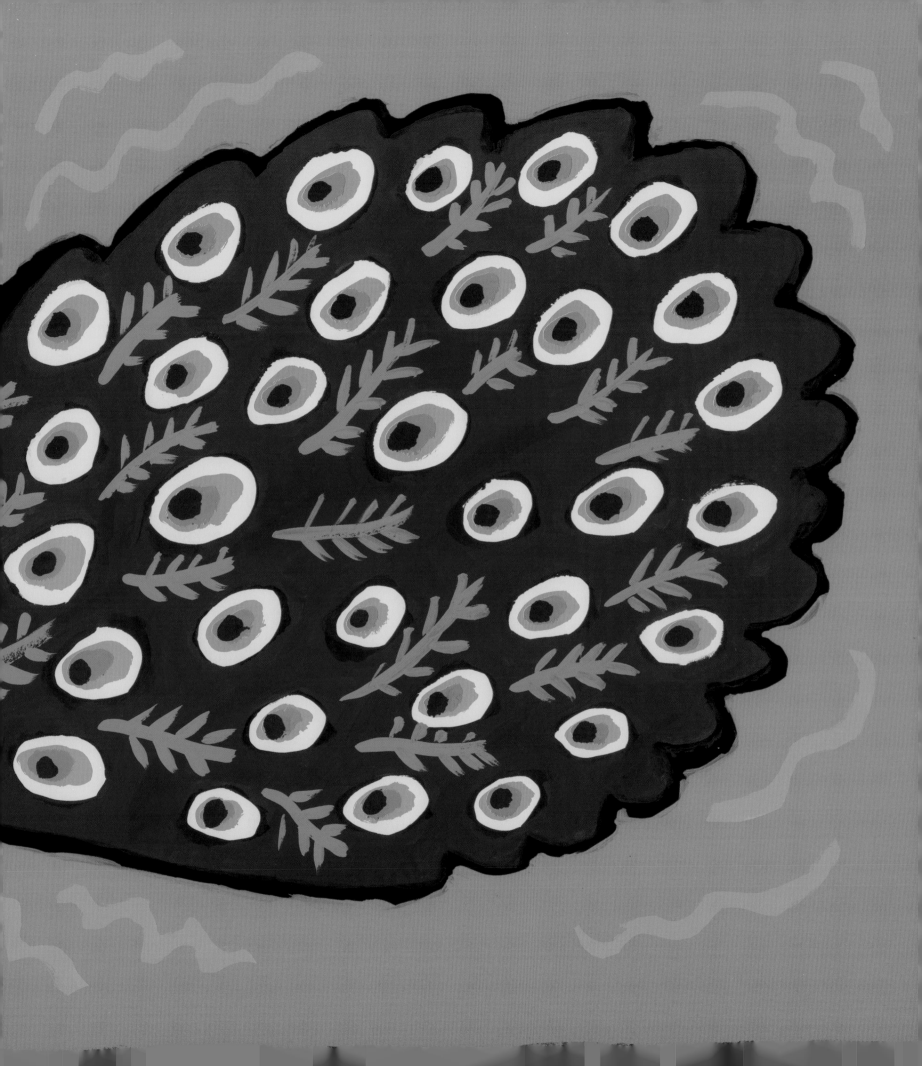

Now sit in your
nest
and cuddle with
Mum.

What a busy bird
you've been.
The funniest one
I've ever seen!

You began the day
Cock-a-doodle-doo!
Now say goodnight...

Lucy Cousins

is the multi-award-winning creator of much-loved character Maisy.
She has written and illustrated over 200 books and has sold
over 37 million copies worldwide.

978-1-4063-3579-8

978-1-4063-8408-6

978-1-4063-3838-6

978-1-4063-4501-8

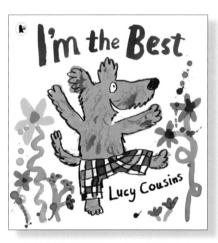

978-1-4063-2965-0

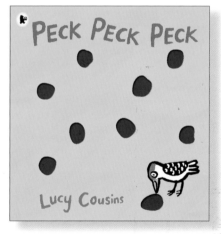

978-1-4063-5547-5

Available from all good booksellers

www.walker.co.uk